not next time, it's scary

Aditya Chatterjee

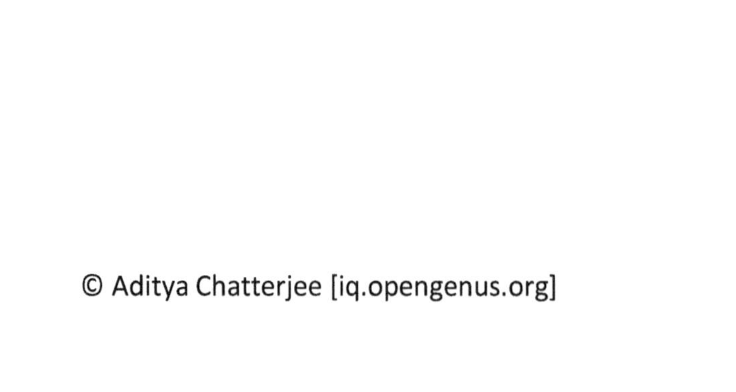

Not Next Time, it's scary.

#1: Perelman's letter

#2: Fired but why?

#3: Back with Tea

#4: Not Next Time

#1: Perelman's letter

42-year-old Chatterjee was coming back from the Market with a bag of sweet potatoes early morning.

Someone was following him.

The person had a satchel and a camera in hand. He walked on his own way ignoring the person, but he knew deep within him that he should reach home fast.

He walked past Mr. Roy who was checking the oil and gear box of his bus to drive the kids of the society to school. Chatterjee greeted "Good day" first time in last 2 years. Roy nodded in surprise.

On reaching home, he screamed "These journalists won't leave me alone".

It was not going to be a normal day. Chatterjee found a letter inside his letter box. It was from Saint Petersburg in Russia. Had it been 15 years back, it would have made sense to people around him.

Nevertheless, he took his morning tea and started to open the envelope. It was a reply from Perelman to Chatterjee's letter sent 19 months back. Tea was kept side and he moved his complete focus on reading through the letter.

The first line read: "I read through your 18 pages. I would say I wasted my time."

Still calm and motivated to get better news, he thought "Perelman would not bother replying if he did not see the value. I should keep reading carefully. I have nothing to lose."

He read through the letter.

Perelman wrote "You send me this equation. You said it to be an approximation to N^{th} solution to Sierpinski's Conjecture with an error less than 5%". It drove my interest initially but I, quickly, found a major flaw. It had a conflict with the proven Henky Flow theory.

I disposed your letter at the point."

Had he been in front of Perelman, he would have asked his opinion on some of the properties of his work but for now, he kept his focus.

Perelman wrote further: "But today after a year, one of my co-researchers arrived at a result that looked familiar to me. It was on your paper and for this, Riesel had to spend weeks to get your letter from our University dump."

"I cannot offer you a job. Reasons you know better but I invite you to visit me at my home at Saint Petersburg. I will host you personally and we will work on some problems."

"Enclosed is the telephone number of Riesel. You can contact him."

Chatterjee took a deep breath, kept the letter into his box of letters and went to his small garden to check his mushrooms.

While having lunch with his Mother, he brought up the conversation about the letter.

Chatterjee: "I heard back from Perelman from Russia. He wants me to come to his place."

Mother: "It will be far away, but it will be a new beginning."

Chatterjee: "I don't think I need his help. He seems interested in the heuristics I formulated to capture how solid body change shape in low gravitational field. With this, we can turn any material into a computing device."

[silence]

Chatterjee: "He will not pay."

Mother: "They may offer you a job at the University later. I have a feeling it will be good. It has been 16 years since you held a job."

Chatterjee: "I do not want to leave you alone here"

Mother: "Once everything falls into place in Russia, you can take me with you. We can hardly make ends meet nowadays. This nation does not recognize your place but may be, in Russia, we can make a fresh start and live happily."

Chatterjee: "I am not sure how it will work out, but I will call his assistant tomorrow and see."

After lunch, Chatterjee returned to his garden to bake under the sun.

#2: Fired but why?

22nd June 1974. An iconic day in history.

Indian Space Organization (ISO) launched a satellite into space with a mission to orbit Jupiter and direct collected energy back to Earth for an indefinite amount of time.

The first of its kind.

Chatterjee led the mission and was the key scientist who designed the path to be taken and was the driving force to solving some of the most challenging blockers.

For the public, he became a National Hero overnight.

He was coming back to his Office in his Ambassador after receiving recognition from Giri, the President of India. He was nominated for Bharat Ratna, the highest Civilian award in India.

He was accompanied by Rao, his junior in his way back.

Rao: "Our satellite will reach Jupiter in 34 days. What will we do with the received energy?"

Chatterjee: "The exact use will depend upon the Government, but I see it as a weaker alternative to our Sun. Today, if the sky is not clear, we cannot harness solar energy to the fullest but if we deploy a satellite around our Earth, we can capture energy from our new source any time."

Rao: "Indeed a futuristic energy source"

Chatterjee: "I see our Moon to do a similar function in a precise way. Had we been very advanced, I would have suspected Moon to have been adjusted by us. Nevertheless, the ability to adjust Earthly bodies in our Solar System is crucial for long term survival."

Rao: "We may not run out of energy source with these advancements but what is your next personal goal?".

Chatterjee: "Life is too short for me to have a goal. It is Humanity who have a direction. Anyways, we have reached Office. I will head towards my cabin."

19 days later, a meteoroid crashed into the satellite and contact was lost. The team was shocked.

Fasir, Director of ISO, was upset at the enormous loss of National resources and had to acknowledge the accident at International level.

Next day, Chatterjee was informed that his nomination for Bharat Ratna was revoked. Later the same day, he was called in for a meeting with Fasir and Giri.

Fasir: "So, do you have an excuse?"

Chatterjee: "It was not exactly a failure. We have 19 days of data which we …"

Giri: "As a face of our country, I am responsible for the loss of public wealth. If we do not get something from a huge investment, it takes our country several years back."

Chatterjee: "I understand."

Giri: "So, the event occurred due to your lack of panning. Right?"

Chatterjee: "It is more of a lack of technology and no one can do it right now. As I explained to Fasir today morning, we should launch an investigation into space activity by other countries.

Fasir: "I heard enough of this excuse."

Giri: "Can it be a national threat?"

Fasir: "No, it just a meteoroid. This incompetent scientist thinks the space is clean."

Chatterjee: "I can say it was not natural."

Fasir: "You are fired. Just leave. Take my advice and leave this profession for good."

Chatterjee leaves the building. Any other person would think of not returning but little was known that he cannot come back ever.

It was clear by the events that followed in the next few days.

Had everything would have happened as expected, India would have been at the forefront of Space exploration and renewal energy source. It was a National loss and personal loss for Chatterjee.

This was a turning point in Indian Space History not only in the career of Chatterjee.

#3: Back with Tea

It is 1983. Chatterjee is still unemployed.

Radhakrishnan, who was his co-worker at Indian Space Organization, came up uninvited at his house. Chatterjee was not surprised as he was expecting someone for years. They sat on the small garden.

Radhakrishnan: "So, how is life going?"

Chatterjee: "Life is great as always. Let us get straight to the point. I, also, need to pick my mushrooms."

Radhakrishnan: "Things did not go smooth at ISO after you left. I remember the countless discussions we had during lunch and can bet on your capability more than anything else. If I were the Chair, I would bring you back."

Chatterjee: "I won't come back."

Radhakrishnan: "Yes, I know you well. I have left ISO last month. What went wrong on that day?"

Chatterjee: "Everyone must be knowing. Don't you?"

Radhakrishnan: "I know that our satellite collided with an unknown object. It was none of our fault, but I suspect you know more than what others do."

Chatterjee: "It was not a meteoroid. It was an object travelling at a small fraction of the speed of light. At least, this is what I saw on my last day when I was analyzing the captured data. It is undefined and no one wants to recognize the actual situation."

Radhakrishnan: "You mean it could be a weapon like object and that too artificially built?"

Chatterjee: "No. I never said so even to Fasir and Giri. It can occur naturally, but it needs more investigation. We had built the system in our satellite to avoid obstacles but in this case, the reaction time was so less that the calculation of the next move could not be computed in time and it collided."

Radhakrishnan: "Can we do it today?"

Chatterjee: "No but based on theoretical limits of the implied calculations, we can achieve it. I studied it. It is one of the most challenging unsolved problems in Computing today."

Radhakrishnan: "By how much were our calculations slow?"

Chatterjee: "Significant. The problem is that today, we need N^2 steps to multiple two N bit numbers and this is the central component in computing moves in such situations quickly."

Chatterjee pulled out a notepad from his paper and started scribbling.

He explained the problem:

Today, the best computers compute at the rate of 10^7 operations per second. The minimum size of data for such situations with reasonable error rate is 10^3 bits.

With this, we need 10^6 operations to multiple the numbers and this results in 0.1 second of computing. The minimum reaction time for the satellite hardware will be around 0.03 seconds today. At our time, it was 0.07 seconds.

We have at the most 0.05 seconds to react in such situations.

I strongly believe we can do the multiplication in N log N operations and this will bring the number of operations to 4 x 10^4 which is roughly 10^{-3} seconds.

4 years back, I had a short telephonic discussion with Knuth. He expressed his thoughts on the problem. It is widely accepted that the best we can do is N log N operations, but it has not been practical realized.

After a long pause, Radhakrishnan said "I know you well enough to say that you still working on this."

Chatterjee replied: "I will solve this once and for all."

Radhakrishnan and Chatterjee went out for a short stroll and revived their old memories when they were young and used to sit among the cows and imagined taking the cows to Mars to start a new thriving community.

The path life took for both was far from what they had
imagined once.

They planned to go out on a short tour to Kadmat
Island in Lakshadweep with their family together next
month. For Chatterjee, I was going to be the most
social thing he had done in last decade.

#4: Not Next Time

"Come fast, how many times do I need to call you?"
shouted Mom.

It was already 5:00PM and we needed to leave to reach
home before it gets dark.

I pulled out the first page from the box of letters I
found. It seems to be a TODO list.

The first line caught my attention:

"Solve Multiplication in N log N: [DONE]"

So, did he solve the challenging problem he mentioned
in the previous letter? Definitely, he did and the
paper with the details must be among this bunch of
papers.

I was exciting to find the paper and go through the
details and see if I can wrap my head around the
discovery that was once out of reach for everyone on
our Planet.

The next few lines had no update:

"Post findings to Perelman: [**] (todo: 27**th
March 2001)

  Remind Berkel to publish ChatteFlow theory [**] (4
months passed)**

  ~~**Meet Radhakrishnan with the findings: [**   **]**~~

  Reply to Romanian Space Agency: [   ] (do by
7th April 2001)

 Collect my pen from Radhakrishnan's home: [   ]"

I wonder why the tasks are not marked. Maybe he missed
ticking the tasks off.

The last line in the list was:

"Get Trinitite from Maximilian: [Collected]"

My attention went to the stone that was stuck among
the papers. It was a glassy stone and had a weird
texture. It seemed some greenery was trapped within
the stone. It was the only stone in the box and is
possibly the trinitite that Chatterjee collected.

Mom came up and demanded that I come down right at that moment. She asked what I was doing.

I reply in hurry: "I am just going through the letters in this box. It seems to be belonged to Uncle Chatterjee."

Mom replied in dismay: "It has been 19 years since he went missing. He was about to be recognized as one of the greatest Scientists in Indian History, but I do not see his name anywhere."

I asked: "What happened to him?"

Mom replied: "As far as I heard from your father, his biggest mission failed, and no one knows what he used to do in the last 25 years when he was living here with his Mother."

After a deep pause:

Mom said: "Anyways, you should not open anything out of the blue. Keep it back where it was and come now."

I closed the box and moved it inside the old wooden cupboard. Without the knowledge of my Mother, I took the stone and kept it inside my pocket.

We left Chatterjee' house.

On our way back home in our car, I asked my Father about Chatterjee.

I asked: "Have you met Chatterjee uncle?"

Father: "Yes, I was at your age when I last met him. I would say he was a genius just not recognized."

Me: "Do you know where he went?"

Father: "Nope, he went missing early 2001. He never returned."

Mom: "What was the letter you found at Post Office?"

Father: "Yes, Chatterjee sent a letter to his Mother sometime in April 2001 saying that he was in hospital and will come in a week. Sad that it was never delivered."

Mom: "So, his Mother checked in the hospital?"

Father: "She could not as the letter was never delivered. Today morning, I went to the Post Office to assist his Mother in some official registration and it was then, that they located the pending letter."

Mom: "I thought Post Office takes a few months to deliver but actually, they can take decades."

Father: "Yeah, they said that address was written on the right side instead of left, so they held it back."

Me: "We can check the Hospital records."

Father: "The hospital does not exist today. We have requested the Police to track down the files.

The strange part is in the letter he talked about some critical invention and asked his Mother not to hand over anything to anyone."

Mom: "I wonder what happened?"

We reached home.

How strange our World is? Chatterjee went missed 2 decades ago and his letter which he sent then is being received now.

I should not have taken his stone and disturbed his stuff.

I wonder what happened to Chatterjee. All answers must be in the box of letters. He was not what others thought him to be.

I need to go back.

Chatterjee will come back, but can he?

Life changes but we must keep walking.